# Inside a House That Is Haunted

## A Rebus Read-Along Story

# Inside a House That Is Haunted

## A Rebus Read-Along Story

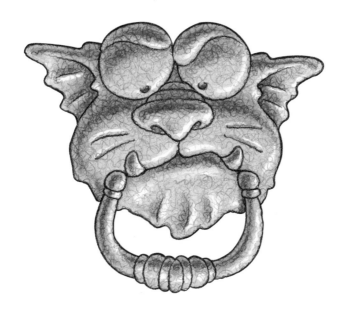

by Alyssa Satin Capucilli
Illustrated by Tedd Arnold

Cartwheel
·B·O·O·K·S·®

SCHOLASTIC INC.
New York   Toronto   London   Auckland   Sydney
Mexico City   New Delhi   Hong Kong

ISBN 0-590-16362-0

Text copyright © 1998 by Alyssa Capucilli.
Illustrations copyright © 1998 by Tedd Arnold.
All rights reserved.
Published by Scholastic Inc. CARTWHEEL BOOKS
and the CARTWHEEL BOOK logo are trademarks and/or
registered trademarks of Scholastic Inc.

12 11 10 9 8 7 6 5 4 3 2 1          9/9 0 1 2 3 4/0

Printed in the U.S.A.                24

First Scholastic paperback printing, October 1999

*For Billy with love*
    *—A.S.C.*

*To Matthew, Justin, and Joshua*
    *—T.A.*

**H**ere is a house that is haunted.

Here is the hand that knocked
on the door
outside a house that is haunted.

Here is the  that knocked
on the door

and startled the spider that
dropped to the floor
inside a house that is haunted.

Here is the  that knocked
on the door
and startled the that
dropped to the floor

that frightened the ghost who
awoke and cried, "BOO!"
inside a house that is haunted.

Here is the  that knocked
on the door
and startled the that
dropped to the floor
that frightened the who
awoke and cried, "BOO!"

surprising the cat that
jumped and screeched, "MEW!"
inside a house that is haunted.

Here is the  that knocked
on the door
and startled the  that
dropped to the floor
that frightened the  who
awoke and cried, "BOO!"
surprising the  that
jumped and screeched, "MEW!"

that shook up the bats that
swooped through the air
inside a house that is haunted.

Here is the  that knocked
on the door
and startled the 🕷 that
dropped to the floor
that frightened the 👻 who
awoke and cried, "BOO!"
surprising the 🐱 that
jumped and screeched, "MEW!"
that shook up the 🦇 that
swooped through the air

and jolted the owl that called,
"Who-Who's there?"
inside a house that is haunted.

Here is the  that knocked
on the door
and startled the that
dropped to the floor
that frightened the who
awoke and cried, "BOO!"
surprising the that
jumped and screeched, "MEW!"
that shook up the that
swooped through the air
and jolted the that
called, "Who-Who's there?"

that spooked the mummy who
ran with a shriek
inside a house that is haunted.

Here is the that knocked
on the door
and startled the that
dropped to the floor
that frightened the who
awoke and cried, "BOO!"
surprising the that
jumped and screeched, "MEW!"
that shook up the that
swooped through the air
and jolted the that
called, "Who-Who's there?"
that spooked the who
ran with a shriek

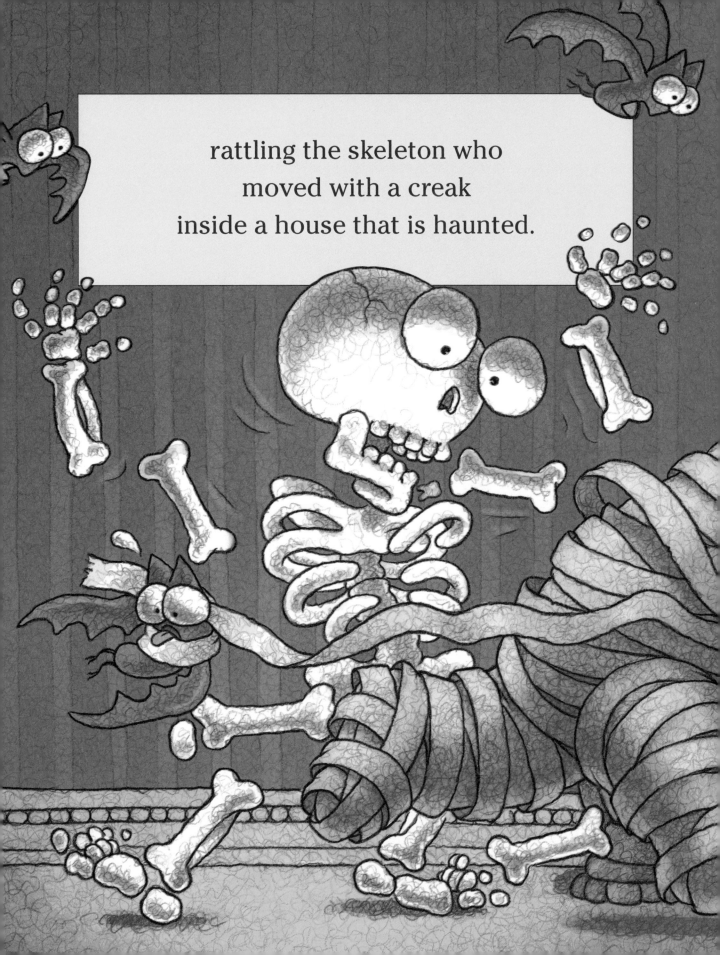

rattling the skeleton who
moved with a creak
inside a house that is haunted.

Here is the  that knocked
on the door
and startled the that
dropped to the floor
that frightened the who
awoke and cried, "BOO!"
surprising the that
jumped and screeched, "MEW!"
that shook up the that
swooped through the air
and jolted the that
called, "Who-Who's there?"
that spooked the who
ran with a shriek
rattling the who
moved with a creak

that woke the monster

inside a house that is haunted.